The Long Trip

A story to help children with stress by recognizing the
power of positive thinking

Diane Schute & Gail Marshall

Published by Schumar Publishing
ISBN: 978-0-692-98181-8
Library of Congress Control Number: 2017918115
The Long Trip | Diane Schute & Gail Marshall
Available formats: Paperback

DEDICATION

To the three people who have helped me think positive thoughts even when the clouds of negativity appear. Their ray of light shines through the clouds and makes life full of sunshine and warmth. Thank you Chaz, Zak, and Bella. Without the three of you, my life would be full of cloudy days. - *D.S.*

Dedicated to Nancy, lifelong friend and passionate educator, who fostered a love of reading and learning in her students, and whose optimism made every day brighter. Her encouragement and positivity brought out the best in all of us. - *G.M*

It was a perfect beach day. The sand stretched to the ocean, which sparkled like glittering jewels. The sun smiled down on the children laughing and splashing in the waves. A little boy and girl played by the water's edge, building sand castles and seeking treasures. Little did they know, there was a whole world living just beyond the sand, a world of ocean creatures, plants, and shells.

At the same time as the children were playing, the ocean world was busy. Colorful fish swam, while creatures living in shells floated by or rested on the ocean floor. Plants waved to each other in the moving water. From time to time, fish would snack on a plant or smaller creature.

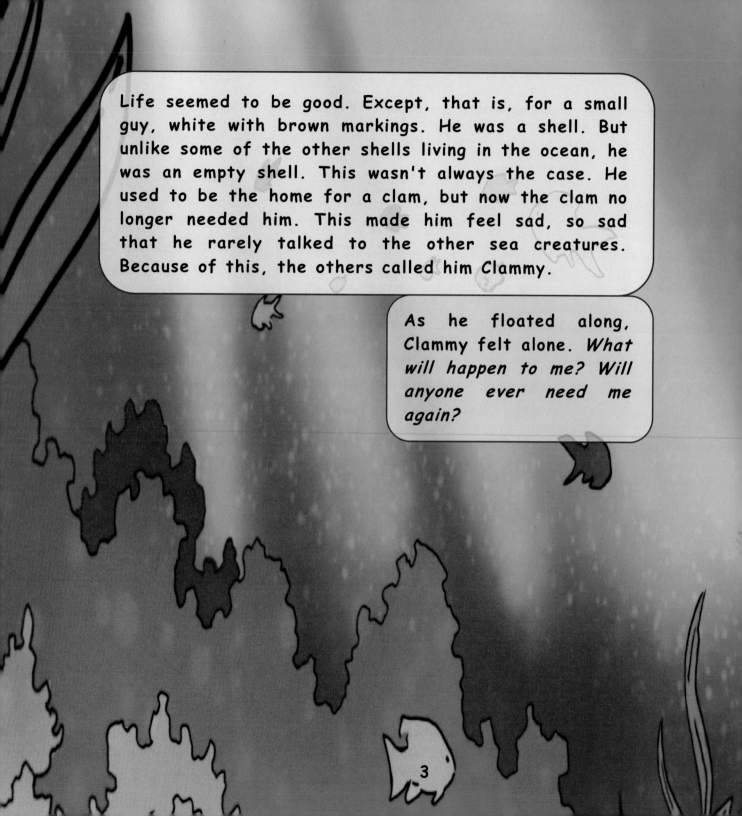

Life seemed to be good. Except, that is, for a small guy, white with brown markings. He was a shell. But unlike some of the other shells living in the ocean, he was an empty shell. This wasn't always the case. He used to be the home for a clam, but now the clam no longer needed him. This made him feel sad, so sad that he rarely talked to the other sea creatures. Because of this, the others called him Clammy.

As he floated along, Clammy felt alone. *What will happen to me? Will anyone ever need me again?*

3

Clammy glanced at the other sea creatures. Some scurried back and forth playing tag. Several fish darted among the rocks in a game of Hide and Seek. Clammy sighed. It seemed like everyone else had friends. As he drifted closer to the bottom of the ocean floor, colorful shells of various shapes and sizes floated by in groups.

The shells told him scary stories of a long trip...and that many shells who take this trip end up broken at the end. A spotted shell showed Clammy a broken edge on his back. Clammy was confused.

What trip? Broken pieces? Ouch! When is this trip? Is this going to happen to me? He shivered.

As the shells drifted away, an old snail's shell floated up to Clammy. He looked very old but beautiful. He was several shades of orange and was twisted into a curled shape with a small hole at the end. He had some chips on his shell.

"Hey kid," he said. "My name's Rusty. I haven't seen you around these parts. What's your name?"

Hello, Rusty, my name is..." Clammy gulped. "I don't really have a name. Nobody gave me one. But the others call me Clammy."

As he thought about how alone he was, a tear slid down his shell.

Rusty smiled and said, "Don't worry, kiddo, you will have a special name one day if you're lucky."

He told Clammy he had gotten his own name a long time ago on the beach from a little boy, before he was swept back out to sea on a wave.

"Named me Rusty...look at me. I'm old. I'm orange. Some imagination with this name, huh?"

This reminded Clammy about the trip. As he asked Rusty about it, Clammy's mouth trembled. Rusty told him not to listen to all of those silly shells. **"Some shells spend their whole lives thinking about all the bad things that could happen. They don't take the time to see all the good things around them. Think positive, happy thoughts and good things will happen."**

Rusty told Clammy that the trip happens often in the ocean, and he explained about tides. He said, "This trip can be difficult, and some shells want to give up, but if you are strong and think positive thoughts, it will be worth the ride!"

When they said goodbye, Rusty smiled. "See ya, kid, till we meet again!"

After Rusty left, Clammy started to feel better. *Maybe those shells were wrong,* he hoped. Rusty's words gave Clammy the courage to look forward to his future instead of feeling so scared.

Just then, Clammy felt a strong push and started to float. *Here I go!* he thought. *This must be what they were talking about.* He squeezed his eyes shut tight and braced himself. He heard shells screaming and the sounds of breaking as they bumped into each other. Clammy rushed by shells, plants, and fish. He felt himself slam into something hard. Ouch! His eyes popped open. It was a large rock. For a few minutes, it felt like he was bouncing from one rock to another like a ping pong ball. He tried to grab onto a green plant as he spun by, but everything was happening too fast. The beautiful colors of a coral reef sped by, but Clammy could not stop to find shelter there.

14

HA HA HA

Clammy closed his eyes and tried to think of the words that Rusty had told him, **"Think positive, happy thoughts and good things will happen."**

So he did. He imagined himself being lifted to a special place full of laughter and beautiful colors. He pictured himself somewhere safe where he could stay and not have to float anywhere else again. He imagined someone special who would need him.

15

All of a sudden, Clammy felt a giant push on his back and then he landed on a soft dry spot. It was so bright, he could hardly make out where he was. Finally he realized the long trip was over. Clammy was on the beach.

He saw some scary things around him. Many broken shells were scattered on this beach. Clammy checked himself all over. He gasped when he noticed a chip in his shell. He started to tear up again, then he remembered Rusty's **words**...

"Relax and remember some shells spend their whole lives thinking of all the bad things in life that could happen. Think positive thoughts and good things will happen."

With that, Clammy looked around and tried to find good things. That is when he noticed many whole shells, beautiful and sparkling. He looked up and saw blue skies that seemed to go on forever. He heard the sounds of children laughing and the ocean behind him sounding like it was saying...YOU MADE IT! YOU MADE IT!

18

19

Still, Clammy couldn't help but wonder what would happen to him. He missed Rusty and worried that he would be swept back into the ocean without getting a name. He was afraid he would be all alone.

Clammy started to get that feeling again and closed his eyes so he could see Rusty and hear him say these words: "Remember, think positive thoughts. Don't waste time thinking about all the bad things that could happen. Think positive, happy thoughts and good things will happen."

Clammy opened his eyes and suddenly realized he hadn't just imagined those words. There was Rusty, in one piece and beaming at him. "Hey, kid, there you are. You made it! Lookin' good!" He winked at Clammy.

"Rusty, you're okay!" shouted Clammy. "I'm so glad to see you. You were right. The trip was scary, but I thought about happy things!"

Suddenly a hand plunged into the water along the sand and snatched Rusty up. "Bella, this one's cool," said the little boy. "It's a keeper."

"I want one too, Zak!" Bella looked around her at all the shells. Finally, she reached down. Clammy felt a rush of air as he was swept up. "This shell is different. And it has a chip on it, just like my tooth! It's not perfect, but it's perfect for me. Hmm…" she said to Clammy. "I think you need a name."

Clammy couldn't believe his ears. *Did she say a name? I'm going to have a real name! No more Clammy!* He puffed up with pride.

Clammy's dreams were coming true. *Rusty was right!* **Thinking positive, happy thoughts works**!

24

Bella said, "You look like a...Sammy. Sammy, I will always keep you with me. When I'm feeling sad or alone or scared, I will hold you and think of the day I found you. I will remember the sounds and smells of the ocean, and I'll feel relaxed and happy."

Sammy, who loved his new name, said to himself, "I will always be there for you, too, Bella. To hold when you are scared, sad, or alone, **helping you think happy thoughts and see good things in life.**"

Bella held Sammy close. Sammy took a deep breath, feeling relaxed and safe. *I have a name and a home and people who love me!* He looked at Rusty and with a wink said, "Life is good!"

The End

Made in the USA
San Bernardino, CA
19 December 2017